W9-BNN-886

**To Blake and Sam – J. W.**
**For my friend Jane – C. B.**

Barefoot Books, 3 Bow Street, 3rd Floor, Cambridge, MA 02138

Text copyright © 2002 by Jakki Wood. Illustrations copyright © 2002 by Clare Beaton
The moral right of Jakki Wood to be identified as the author and Clare Beaton to be
identified as the illustrator of this work has been asserted

This book is printed on 100% acid-free paper
This book was typeset in Plantin Schoolbook Bold 20 on 28 point
The illustrations were prepared in felt with braid, beads and sequins
Graphic design by Judy Linard, England. Color separation by Grafiscan, Italy
Color transparencies by Jonathan Fisher Photography, Bath
Printed and bound in Singapore by Tien Wah Prss Pte Ltd.

Library of Congress Cataloging-in-Publication Data
Wood, Jakki.
    Never say boo to a goose! / written by Jakki Wood ; illustrated by Clare Beaton. -1st ed.
    [24] p. : col. ill. ;   cm.
    Summary: A pesky little kitten learns a big lesson as he journeys around the farmyard,
trying to put his mother's advice of "Never say 'Boo' to a goose" to the test.
    ISBN 1-84148-255-2
    1. Cats - Fiction.  2. Geese - Fiction.  2. Animals - Fiction.  I. Beaton, Clare. II. Title.
    [E] 21  2002   AC   CIP        1 3 5 7 9 8 6 4 2

"I'll never say 'Boo!' to a goose again."

"Hiss! Honk! Hiss!"

"YIKES! I'm getting out of here."

"This is hopeless ... Excuse me, have you seen a goose around here?"
"Well, yes, I am a goose."

"Hello. Are you a goose?"
"Whoever heard of a goose with a woolly coat? Baaa, baaa, baaa, you silly little kitten. I'm a sheep."

"Boo, all you gooses!"
"Gooses ... gooses? Do you mean geese? We aren't geese, we're pigs and piglets. Oink, oink, oink."

"Woof, woof, woof!"
"Oh, oh, he's not a goose. He's that noisy dog, Growler.
I'm not going to say 'Boo!' to him."

"Boo, goose!"
"Quack, quack, quack. Who do you think
you are calling a goose? I'm a duck."

"I wonder who you are. Boo, goose!"
"Hee-haw, hee-haw! You silly little kitten. Does a goose have four legs, and long fluffy ears? I'm not a goose, I'm a donkey."

"Pesky birds! I'll show them. Boo, goose!"
"Cluck, cluck, cluck. Silly kitten. We're not geese, we're hens."

All the kittens listened carefully. But Tiger took no notice. "Why can't I say 'Boo!' to a goose?" he thought. "I can say 'Boo!' to anyone I like." And off he went.

"You can go anywhere in the farmyard," said Mother Cat to her kittens, "but be careful of the dogs. And whatever you do, never say 'Boo!' to a goose."

# Never Say
# BOO
# to a Goose!

written by **Jakki Wood**

*illustrated by* **Clare Beaton**

**Barefoot Books**
*Celebrating Art and Story*

# Barefoot Books
*Celebrating Art and Story*

At Barefoot Books, we celebrate art and story
with books that open the hearts and minds of children
from all walks of life, inspiring them to read deeper,
search further, and explore their own creative gifts.
Taking our inspiration from many different cultures,
we focus on themes that encourage independence of
spirit, enthusiasm for learning, and acceptance of
other traditions. Thoughtfully prepared by writers,
artists and storytellers from all over the world, our
products combine the best of the present with the
best of the past to educate our children as the
caretakers of tomorrow.

*www.barefootbooks.com*